# The Cure

# The Cure

*. . . and the Story of Anana's Slavery*

F. David Raymond, Sr.

iUniverse, Inc.
Bloomington

**The Cure**
**. . . and the Story of Anana's Slavery**



iUniverse books may be ordered through booksellers or by contacting:

iUniverse
1663 Liberty Drive
Bloomington, IN 47403
www.iuniverse.com
1-800-Authors (1-800-288-4677)



ISBN: 978-1-4620-5983-6 (sc)
ISBN: 978-1-4620-5982-9 (ebk)

Printed in the United States of America

iUniverse rev. date: 10/12/2011

# 1—Dead L. A. Prostitute

It is a warm June night in 2008. Mandisa Jones is walking her regular 'beat'. She walks up to a car and gets in. Mandisa and her customer go to a hotel nearby, do some drugs, and engage in sex. 'John' asks if he can stay the night and she's happy to have a customer for the whole evening—and the pay is good.

They inject some more drugs and go to sleep.

In the morning, he wakes up and finds her lying in bed with her eyes open and her mouth covered in dry foam. Of course he doesn't try to do CPR or even call 911. He panics and leaves.

Later that day, her body is discovered by the maid. The police send her body to a hospital and everything is routine with their investigation. But, everything is not normal.

In the morgue, the doctors are talking to the detective who came in to close the case.

"Lieutenant Johnson, we have an interesting case here," Sandra Arnold said. "Your guys last night said that this prostitute has a long record has been on the street since she was about sixteen."

Johnson replied, "Yep. I arrested her over ten years ago the first time and a few since then. She is a regular. What are you going to tell me, she is riddled with AIDS, syphilis and had a cold? Hell, by now she should have been dead 5 years."

Sandra continued, "That's the interesting thing. She doesn't appear to have any illness. Look at her." She pulled back the sheet to show a fine specimen of a 30 year-old, well-conditioned and healthy native African woman. "She should show some signs of some disease by now."

"Well, I guess she just kept herself in shape. I don't see anything unordinary. We have her as a drug overdose. Her 'john' is unknown and the room was in her name. Treat her as an indigent and send her body for cremation."

"But, what about her relatives?" Sandra asked.

"She has none. Believe me Doctor," Johnson said, "we know Mandisa. She has no one and no one cares about her. We—the social workers—have done everything to get her a job and to straighten her out. Something was wrong with her and we had no way to find any relatives. She told us once that all of her relatives died in Angola. Just send her to the furnace, I have paperwork to do."

Doctor Arnold nodded yes and Lt. Johnson left. But, before turning her over to the technicians, Sandra took some blood—just three tubes. She wanted to send them for tests. This beautiful young woman had to be disease-ridden and was not. "How could she appear so healthy after 16 years on the street?"

---

# 2—The Lab

A delivery girl drops off the lab requests to the morgue's pathology department. The note from Dr. Arnold that is wrapped around the three tubes reads: 'Run this through as many tests as you can, when you get time. The patient was a prostitute for 16 years and showed no outward signs of any disease. I'm just curious.'

The technician put the tubes and the blood in the refrigerator and sat down to work on more pressing issues.

A week later, another technician takes out the tray and reads the note. She frowns and puts the tray back, but she bangs the tray on the shelf and one tube drops out. It breaks when it hit's the floor. The tray is put in place and the floor is cleaned.

Another week passes and the two techs are sitting with little to do. It is mid-July and very hot outside, there is little crime.

The first technician decided to clean the fridge and notices that there is a tube missing. "Ratree, there is a tube of blood missing from this tray. Do you know where it is?" Lynette asked.

Ratree looked up from her magazine and replied, "Oh, I accidentally broke it. Since I read the note and saw there were no issues involved, I just cleaned it up."

Lynette replied, "Well, it is kind of slow, why don't we run the tests?"

"Okay."

They started to run all the standard tests and all the results were negative. This dead prostitute had absolutely no adverse medical condition.

"How can this girl pass an 'Elisa' test?" Ratree asked. "She was a whore for 14 years and we haven't found a single abnormality in her blood."

"Disease? I haven't found any trace of drugs in her blood either," Lynette added. "If she was a baby, this blood would be normal. I think we need to send this to the medical center."

The ladies prepared their report and sent the two remaining tubes (1/3 full) and the test results to the LA County/USC Medical Center.

The technician who accepted the package read it and took it to the Chief Pathologist. Dr. Rodriguez was intrigued and stated, "Take this to our lab school and tell them to tell me what is going on."

A few days later, the Senior Instructor (Dr. Carlson) tells one of the students to do reverse tests on the remaining blood. "Put the disease into the blood and let's see what happens."

Within 30 minutes, the students send a fellow to get the instructor. He runs quickly and doesn't even bother to knock. He quickly says something to the director and they leave in a hurry.

Dr. Carlson looks in the microscope and looks at the video records. "My God!!! What have we found?"

Less than an hour later, he is presenting his findings to the Medical Center's senior pathologists. "Gentlemen, look at this reaction. We inject syphilis into the blood and the disease was ignored by the red blood cells and destroyed immediately by the white blood cells. We introduced herpes and got the same result. We then introduced HIV and . . . . see for yourself . . . ." The screen showed the immediate destruction of all HIV cells by the WBCs. "Gentlemen, we may have found the cure for AIDS and every other sexually transmitted disease. Hell, we may have the cure for cancer!"

Dr. Rodriguez broke in, "Let's do some more research and duplicate the experiments. Make sure we do at least three tests on each disease and film all the results. I'm going to find the patient this blood came from. And, I mean this very seriously, do not talk to anyone about this."

He turned to Dr. Carlson and said, "Discuss this anomaly with your students and explain that their silence could be important to their careers as researchers but their talking could result in their failure and dismissal from school."

Dr. Rodriguez is on the phone with the medical center distribution center. He asks, "Can you tell me where the package came from you delivered to me this morning?" He waited and then a look of shock came on his face. "The city morgue? . . . Never mind, thank you."

Rodriguez called the morgue. And said, "This is Dr. Rodriguez, Chief Pathologist. You sent me the strange blood to test?"

Lynette explained to him everything they did and why they sent the blood. She also told him about the third tube that was destroyed.

Rodriguez asked, dejectedly, "and you had the blood two weeks before you tested it?"

"Yes, there was no rush because the deceased was a closed case. We were told to do the tests when we had the time." Lynette offered.

Rodriguez decided to visit the morgue. Dr. Arnold filled him in on the situation as she saw it. She showed him pictures of the patient and he agreed she should have shown some signs of something. But, he wasn't offering any information.

"Who was the detective on this case? You said he knew the woman from past arrests?"

Arnold replied, "Yes, he said he had arrested her a few times and seemed to know about the search for her roots."

"Can you call Johnson and ask him to meet with me? I want both of you to come to my office as soon as you can. And, Dr.

Arnold, this is very important. We need to remain control of who knows about this young woman's blood. Let the ladies in the morgue know that their work is much appreciated and that we are working on a cure for herpes due to their skills. Say no more and tell them to wait for credit and reward. You understand what I am saying?"

"Yes, doctor, I understand. I will call Johnson and we'll get back to you STAT."

---

# 3—The Meeting

Arnold and Johnson are sitting in Rodriguez' office. Rodriguez is on the phone. He hangs up the phone and looks at them.

"Dr. Arnold, your office has come across one of the most significant discoveries in our time. I cannot underscore the magnitude of your findings. We now believe we have a cure for AIDS—or, at least one is out there. This young woman's blood is a miracle. Her blood actually kills the virus. Not only the HIV but all STDs and, at this time, we have not found any disease that can survive in her blood. I believe we are seeing a miracle."

"Lt. Johnson, we need your help. I have not contacted the CDC or any government agency yet. The last thing I want is the government getting involved which would result in media leaks and a circus atmosphere before we know anything for certain."

"That said, Lieutenant, we do know what her blood can resist. But, we need more and we need to find her relatives. Dr. Arnold has told me that you know about her and have known her for many years. We have to find her relatives."

Detective Johnson shook his head, "Doctor Rodriguez, I don't know what to say. This is a great discovery. But, I don't know if I can help. I did know Mandisa for quite a few years. I don't know when she came to America or LA. I do know that the first time I busted her, I was a vice cop and that was ten years ago. We busted her a few times, she spent a short time in jail and she always went back to the street."

He continued, "She participated in our counseling session and worked with the social workers. None of them have ever mentioned any relatives. Can't you just notify INS?

"We could do that," Rodriguez replied, "but we could start something we don't want. If the Chief Pathologist of LA County contacts the INS to find information on one person, there will be a lot of questions. And, they will ask those questions amongst themselves while involving many people from here to DC to Africa."

He continued, "But, if a detective from LAPD contacts the local office and tells them the information is needed to help solve a crime . . . . Well, the questions are answered and the rumors are never started. No one cares about who's involved in crimes, but a medical situation that could affect any number of people? Well, you know how people are."

Lt. Johnson replied, "I see your point. I will see what I can find out."

---

# 4—Rodriquez, Johnson and INS

Lt. Johnson and another man are in Dr. Rodriguez's office. It's been 4 weeks and some situations have arisen. Johnson takes a drink of coffee.

"Dr. Rodriguez, this is Agent Mark Testerman from ICE. He needs to talk with you."

Testerman began "Dr. we need to know what is so special about this case and who needs to know about this woman. As a matter of fact, we would like to talk to her . . ."

Rodriguez interrupted, "Who are you? Why are you looking for this person? And, more importantly, didn't Lt. Johnson tell you the woman died 6 months ago?"

Testerman looked at Johnson. Detective Johnson started, "Hold on! I'll explain to both of you."

"This better be good." Testerman said. "I've come a long way to hear about a dead woman."

Johnson began, "When I started looking for information on Mandisa Jones, I knew I would get nowhere. That is, if the INS or their ICE branch knew she was dead. So, I had to keep her alive. Also, I knew that if I mentioned anything about needing relatives for medical reasons, few in the government would care. So, I came up with a drug and money connection and a need to find her sources in Africa."

Testerman cut in, "you think you have us pegged don't you?"

"Well, you're here. And, it appears to be a priority for ICE." Johnson replied. "Let me continue. After I contacted the LA office of ICE, we found out that Mandisa came to LA about '90 or '91.

We're not sure because the only people who would have known exactly when or why are now buried in Alabama."

"It appears, from our search, that Mandisa and her family were political immigrants from Angola in 1978." Johnson started.

"They were a small group of 10 who all came together with a senior member of the CIA." Testerman volunteered. "It is that connection that got our office's attention. When the CIA took the time to care enough to bring refugees out of an insignificant dispute, we start asking questions. We get no answers and the State Department did not or could not honor our requests. But, we still wonder. That is why we do have the little information we have. But, none of this is official and we don't know where it came from."

"If I may," Johnson broke in, "This group of immigrants all were given new surnames by someone, U.S. citizenship by the State Department, and given money and help in purchasing homes in Dothan, Alabama."

"Basically, there were three couples and four children. Mandisa was one of the kids and she was 2-3 years old. They were 'assigned' birthdates and ages based on what the folks in INS determined they looked like. The birthdays were just randomly picked by the immigrants."

Rodriguez stopped him with an upraised hand. "What does all this get to? I am interested in her family. So, far, I am hearing a lot of past-tense terms."

Johnson continued, "Well, that is the problem. They are all dead."

"All of them?" Rodriguez asked.

"Yes. One couple and their child died in a car accident during a 1981 snowstorm. The older couple moved to Atlanta in '90 to be with their daughter who was starting college. They were killed in a home invasion in '91. Their daughter quit school and returned to Africa . . . ."

"Angola?" Rodriquez inquired.

"No, Zambia." Johnson continued. "That just added to the mystery. But, Mandisa's family seemed to fare better. Her father took the name of Jones—no reason. His name was Abu. That doesn't help us much as that means 'father' in many African dialects. As a matter of fact, Mandisa means 'sweet'. The mother's name was Ummi and, yep, . . . . you guessed it, . . . . that means 'mother'. However, there was a sister. We think she was adopted because her name was Xhosa, which also means 'sweet'. But, here's the twist. Xhosa is a South African name. Why would they name each child the same? I mean, there are very few George Foremans out there."

"Abu died in a '93 fishing accident. Nothing strange. The boat capsized and he and two others drowned. The mother, Ummi, died two years ago and is interred in the same crematorium as her husband—no DNA available."

"Another mystery is what happened to Xhosa. We don't know. It appears as though she and Mandisa left home at the same time. Mandisa came here to LA and Xhosa departed for Zambia. That has been verified by INS. But, if they were from Angola, why did she return to Zambia. Two girls, same group from Angola and she returns to Zambia? That is all I could come up with." Johnson looked at Testerman and took a drink of coffee.

"Well," Testerman picked it up, "that wasn't the end of the story, nor the beginning."

"It appears as though this group was brought to the U.S.A. as immigrants but the details are sketchy. Their arrival seems to have been on a military aircraft with no flight plan. None of the people on board can be located in any of our databases. I mean, even the pilots never existed in our military. This does have CIA stamped all over it. We came to a brick wall."

Rodriguez took the break to ask, "so we can get nowhere on this?"

"Oh, I didn't say that." Testerman smiled. "I have a friend who works with DOD. And, he worked with INS prior to transferring to them. He did some searching and found an 'Operation Hackman' . . . ."

Johnson asked, "You mean like Gene Hackman? What did the DOD do with him?"

"Well, yes and no. It does have a 'French Connection'" (and he used the 'air quotes' we all hate) "and they chose the name because of that."

Rodriguez interrupted, "so these people came from France?"

"No. In the '70s, many countries in Africa were going through political turmoil. Many of these, like Angola, were using mercenaries. As a matter of fact, many of the mercenaries were captured and executed. And, for some reason, a lot of the mercenaries were French. In spite of that, the governments doing the executing swore these killers were Americans."

He stopped, took a drink and continued. My friend has found some of the people involved in the planning of this operation and he wants to have you, Dr. Rodriguez, bring your research with you and meet with key people from the DOD and CIA in Langley. Here are your airplane tickets. I am here to escort you and we leave tomorrow morning. I'll have a car pick you up at 8 at your home."

A week later I get involved.

---

# 5—Impressments?

It was like the beginning of "Stargate"—the first one with Kurt Russell not the TV show. You know, where he's trying to be left alone after his retirement and he is drafted to lead a mission. We've all said it, 'that only happens in the movies.'

Well, we are wrong . . . . it happened to me.

I retired from the Army in the early 90s after I'd gone as far as I could and was young enough to start anew. I used my GI Bill and became a teacher and had a good life. It was now 2009 and I was teaching History in a school I loved in my home state of North Carolina.

One day, I was walking down the hall and saw two older-looking guys dragging one of my students into the bathroom. It didn't look like he wanted to go. And, the assailants did not look young enough to be students. I quickly followed them in and saw what looked like one hitting my student in the stall. I told him to stop and proceeded forward.

The other guy stepped in front of me and put his hand on my chest. No one had touched me in years and it was not a pleasant feeling. I twisted his hand and put him on his knees and when he tried to swing I punched him in the face, which put him out, and moved on. The second one turned my way and lurched at me. I side-stepped him also—tennis comes in handy, elbowed him behind his neck and he went down. Once I saw they were out of the fight, I turned to the 'victim' in the stall.

When I looked in the stall, the 'student' came at me with a knife. I grabbed his wrist and pushed him to the side and slammed my left hand against his elbow. You could hear the snap. He dropped the knife and went down. It was then that I heard the voice . . . .

"Sergeant Major! Stand down!"

This was a command I understood and a voice I recognized. I looked and it was my former commander from my much earlier days. He looked at me and said, "We just wanted to see how much work we had to do. Doesn't look like our job is too hard. You seem to have stayed in shape."

"Colonel Ball? I have two questions," I said. "First, what the hell is going on? Who are these guys? Second, you do understand I have been retired 10 years?"

"Sergeant Major Raven, you have been retired 15 years but and we need you back. And, that was three questions."

Now you have to understand, I thought I was long out of the Army I had not heard my nickname in many years. My last name is Raymond, but I was called 'the Raven' by some old dear friends.

"Please come with me," he continued, "we need to talk." He looked at the other two guys behind him and motioned toward my 'test', "clear these guys out of here."

We found ourselves in the Principal's Office with my principal telling me that he already had a sub and understood that I had to leave. I asked him, "Have they told you anything?" They had not—he shook his head 'no' and said, "Only that it is national security and they need you.

In the car, Colonel Ball corrected me, "I'm a Lieutenant General now and work in a dead-end job in the Pentagon." He continued, "Raven, we need you. A situation has developed and a special request has been made—for you."

---

# 6—The Team

A long time ago, near the end of the Vietnam War—and for all you idiots that call it a 'conflict', it was a war—I entered the Army out of high school. I volunteered to go to and saw a little action in the jungles.

After Congress lost the war and the country voted against Ford and elected the (up until 2009) worst president in history—'Uncle Jimmy'—I was assigned to the 82d Airborne Division. I was happy. I had a good life and got to jump out of perfectly good planes for an extra $55 a month.

Then we had Iran. I hoped that we would have just turned them into a parking lot. But, Jimmy would have none of that . . . like the current Appeaser-in-Chief, he wanted to 'talk' with them. How'd that work out . . . . then and now? But, I'm rambling. I do that. I'm old.

Let me tell you about what was happening in Africa at that time. There were many despots arising and most of them hated the U.S.A.—even though we put them in power. Some of these countries had U. S. military technology. The DOD decided that this equipment had to be neutralized or confiscated—that's a nice way to say destroyed or stolen. So, the DOD—actually, I believe no one in Carter's administration knew of our work—decided to send specialized teams to do the dirty work.

These teams were put together from various units at Fort Bragg. In my team, we had members from the Green Beret, the 82d Infantry and Artillery, a COSCOM intelligence unit and a few guys with long hair from 'the Company'. We all had one thing in common—we spoke French.

Reed and I came from the same company, so we knew each other. There were ten of us, but I only learned the true identities of four other team members, and that was only after a long time and many coincidences. All of the selection process was designed so that no one knew anyone else—if it could be helped—and we could, therefore, not tell anyone under torture what we did not know. Let me tell you what I do know.

Sergeant First Class (SFC) David "Tennessee" Reed, Infantry, 82nd Airborne Division, was a decorated veteran from Vietnam and was a small-arms and demolition specialist. He had served a full year with the French Foreign Legion contingent in Vietnam and his French was very good. Oh, he was from Bristol, Tennessee. He was our team's NCOIC.

SSG Gary "Cat" Kiddy, Infantry, 82nd Airborne Division, had never seen combat but had lived with his parents in Chad when his dad worked at the Embassy. He spoke French fluently. He was a crew-served weapons specialist and a 'genius' with electronics. He would be our communications guy.

SSG Mike "Street" Lane, Infantry, 82nd Airborne Division, saw action in Vietnam from the day before 'Tet' until 1972. He liked it there. His mother was French and he was fluent. He was a motor pool mechanic. Actually, he was the best damn mechanic I ever saw.

Agent Harry "Company" Fuhrman, CIA Operative. That's it. We didn't know anything else except he worked in the Central African section in Langley. He had no formal military experience but had seen a lot of combat in Vietnam and in Cold War action.

Me? I am Robert "Raven" Raymond, Infantry SSG, 82nd Airborne Division. I was trained in small arms and crew served weapons at Fort Polk, LA. My father was French and I grew up speaking it as a second language and 'learned' it in four years of high school French. I saw action in Vietnam in '72-73 for 18 months. I spent 22 years in the Army and retired as a Sergeant Major in 1994.

Green Beret 1LT James "Grunt" Ball was one of the 57 Marines from Delta Company, 1st Battalion, 4th Marines, involved with the assault to free the SS *Mayaguez* in May '75. He had been a young Marine sergeant with two tours in Vietnam and was literally inches away from being the fourth Marine executed by the Khmer Rouge. He left the Marines upon returning to the states, got his degree and entered the U.S. Army in '77 as a First Lieutenant. He was assigned to the Special Forces and received training in French at the Presidio.

None of this I knew at the time. What I knew was that I was a Platoon Sergeant in an Airborne Infantry Company that got a call at 3 AM one morning and reported to my unit for an 'alert'. I was met outside my unit by three military police who told me I needed to come with them for my mission. I asked questions, they didn't answer. I guess you could say that we 'had an understanding'.

They took me to Special Forces Headquarters. I was told to remove my blouse (military shirt) and I was led to a room and the door was opened by the armed Green Beret guarding it and I entered. I sat down and waited. Reed came in and we shook hands and indicated that we were each confused about the situation. Kiddy and Lane entered but we did not introduce ourselves—not much sense because obviously someone did not want us to know other's identities. Four other men came in from the 82nd. Three Green Beret entered and four 'Legs' (non-Airborne soldiers). Fifteen men who had no clue as to what was happening and apparently only two of us knew each other.

Ball and a civilian entered. The civilian was Fuhrman. We did not know what Ball's rank was or what his name was but the Green Beret soldiers stood to attention so we knew he was an officer, we came to attention. He gave as 'at ease' and told us to sit. I guess we were going to learn something.

"Gentlemen, you are all here because you have one skill we need, you are all fluent in French." He continued, "If you do not feel you are fluent, then our records may be incorrect and I need to know now. If you are not, please leave and you will be returned to your unit." Two legs and a paratrooper stated they were passable but not fluent—one said he spoke only Creole. They all left. Twelve men remained.

Ball waited until they exited and continued, "some of you have seen combat and some have not. All of you may be combat veterans when we finish this mission but we are hoping that will not happen. If there is anyone here who does not wish to see action, please leave." A 'leg' got up and stated he was only in the Army for the GI Bill and walked out. Ball stated that he would get orders to the Korean DMZ next week. We laughed. Eleven men remained.

"We need a team that speaks French. You all do. We need specialists in crew served weapons, small arms, demolitions and communications. Is there anyone here that does not feel they are an expert in one of these areas?"

Three men stood up. Ball pointed at Lane and told him to sit down. The other two men were told to leave. Ball told Lane, "You are a mechanic. We may need that skill."

There were now nine men sitting in a room with no knowledge of what was expected of them. Ball looked at one of the Green Berets and told him to stand up. He had him do 20 jumping jacks. When the man finished, he bent over and grabbed his knee.

"I see you haven't recovered from surgery yet. You're dismissed." Ball said. The man said nothing and exited the room.

"You eight men are now part of Team B. There are three 10 man teams. We are your final two team members." Ball said this as he looked at Fuhrman and they nodded at each other. "I am the team leader. My second in command is this man." He pointed at Reed. That is when I knew that we were all enlisted—except Ball. I don't think anyone else knew that.

---

# 7—The Briefing

"You are all part of Operation Hackman. All of you have secret clearances. I will tell you that. From this moment on, that clearance has been elevated to top secret and legal consequences of that classification now apply. Now, exit to the left, go to the fourth door on the right and wait until called."

We went in a room with about 30 other men and waited. There were three doors at the back of the room and each had a light over it. There was one Green Beret Captain standing behind a lectern in the back corner. We could see the lights and where we were designated to sit. The guys in our group who were Green Berets went to the front row and sat down. We followed and sat behind them so we could see what was happening. As a light came on, the Captain pointed at the next man in the front row and they went through the door. No words, just actions.

While sitting there, we observed that the Green Berets were taking out their wallets, taking off their dog tags and removing any rings or watches. No one was wearing any earrings as we were all men. You can take that anyway you want, real men don't wear earrings.

When my time came, I went through the door and saw two open boxes on the left, one medium, one small. The civilian (I assume because he had longer hair and no uniform) behind a desk told me, in French, to put all personal items and/or any item identifying me in the small box. Then he told (everything said was in French) me to remove my uniform and place it in the larger box.

He told me that I would be given another uniform. He asked me if any undergarments had any labels.

"I believe they are fruit of the loom," I replied as I pulled at my brief waistband. "The OD T-shirt and brown socks are Army issued."

He told me to take them all off and pointed at the many boxes on the right. I picked out some underwear and socks and noticed they had French labels on them. Later, I would find out that in the other rooms, the items came from Canada and Niger.

When I finished putting on my skivvies, the man told me to go through the door and finish getting dressed. Upon entering, I noticed that there were many uniform items that looked like they were Canadian. I knew this because the 82nd had a great program of exchanging units with other countries and I had the chance to work with British, Australian, and Canadian soldiers in the last few years. So, I got dressed and put on a new pair of jungle boots.

The 'civilian' sitting in the corner told me (in French) to take two additional pants and shirts and four sets of underwear and socks identical to the ones I was wearing. He pointed at a rucksack. When I finished, he told me to exit.

I entered a hallway and was directed by the Green Beret out there to move down the hall to the left. One man was wearing his skivvies and carrying a box and went past me to the right. Obviously, his French wasn't very good.

Most others exiting the doors were walking with me. As we approached the end of the hall, a 'civilian' stopped us and asked us each a question in French and carried on a 2-3 minute conversation. Most people were directed to his left and one was sent to his right. Another drop-out.

Later, we discovered that the whole French-thing in the changing rooms was a test of our ability to actually converse in French. We estimated that almost 40 men entered the changing rooms and 32 were sitting in the large briefing room an hour later.

After relaxing in the briefing room for a few minutes and starting to doze off—it was now 6 AM by the clock on the wall—I awoke to the sound of an entrance at the front of another civilian. It looked as though we were going to actually learn what was going on. It was about time.

"Gentleman, civil war has been on-going in Angola since '75. Angola got it's independence from Portugal and many would-be leaders have moved in to try to be 'the government'. Most notable amongst these is John Banks, a Briton. He has recruited mercenaries to fight for the *National Front for the Liberation of Angola* (FNLA). The other major group is the *Popular Movement for the Liberation of Angola* (MPLA)."

"We don't care about either of these groups and we don't care who is in charge in that piss-ant country. What we do care about is that there are many stockpiles of U.S. Military equipment there. That is where you come in. We want it back or we want it destroyed."

"Operation Hackman involves three teams. Each of you has been assigned to a ten to twelve person team. (Aside to another man) Those are the current numbers?"

"And, each team has people trained in crew-served weapons. Your job will be to disable these weapons. Since you have the ability to perform operator maintenance, it should not be hard to break what you have been trained to fix."

"Each team has members who are experts in demolitions. Your job will be to destroy anything that cannot be disabled. Remember, disable or destroy. Any vital piece, like firing pins, should be brought back with you . . . or at least dropped in a distant location."

"All of you speak French and all of you will have papers from a country other than the U.S.A. and you will conduct all of your radio communication in French. Effective touch down in Angola, you are mercenaries. The U. S. Government does not know you and there will be no record of your assigned identity ever being in the U.S.A. While you are gone, your parent units will be deployed on FTX (field training exercises) until you return. They do not know where you are and never will know—except you being on Special Duty somewhere on Bragg."

He continued on for a few minutes and all I could think of was the "Mission: Impossible" theme and the 'disavow any knowledge' clause. But he was still talking . . . .

"All of your weapons will be from items the U.S. has sold to three countries—Canada, Belgium and France. Should you be captured, these numbers will indicate where the weapons came from. We have also issued you clothing from those countries. The bottom-line . . . . You are not and never have been American."

"Questions?"

One soldier asked about why we didn't just blow up everything and get out. The response was that if a government friendly to the U.S.A. comes to power, we want to be in a position to help them repair the damage caused by the losers in retreat. We were covering all our bases.

Another question was about our role as combatants and engaging the enemy. If we encounter any force we were to eliminate any knowledge of our being there. If captured by the FNLA or Banks' mercenaries, we are there to capture equipment for our own operation in Uganda. If captured by the MPLA, they will automatically assume you work for Banks. We were told that being captured might result in torture and possible execution.

There were a few more questions and non-answers. We were told that the mission had started and we were going to move to an area north of Gamba, Zaire. This put us as close to the Angolan border as we needed to be. Team Alpha would dispatch to Quibala,

Team Bravo (us) was to move to Luso, and Team Charlie would go to Cuito. The rally point upon completion of the mission was to be Cazombo. This was a small border village near Rhodesia. We could not establish any base in Zambia, but they allowed us to use their airspace and we could land choppers to pick us up.

I was brought out of my thoughts . . . .

“Sergeant Major? Do you remember Cazombo?” asked General Ball.

“Yes, sir, vaguely,” I replied.

“Well, that little ‘vague’ village has become very important,” he continued, “I’ll tell you more on the flight to DC.”

---

# 8—Flight to DC

On the flight, the general gave me a briefing on what had transpired over the last nine months. He told me of Mandisa and Xhosa and their families. I remembered them well. I had fond memories of the families and the two daughters. Both were sweet little girls and I did not find out until later that when I called them sweetheart, I was using their name, 'Sweet'. But, I'm getting ahead of myself.

Ball continued, "A lot has happened since we left there a lifetime ago. Those refugees turned out to be very important. Unfortunately, we just found this out. You remember when we entered Cazombo? The people there were under constant attack by the government troops and guerillas."

He paused. He let my memories drift back and continued, "Well, when we got there, we were the first team to arrive and we had a two day wait for the others . . . . or those that made it out."

He was referring to the fact that three in our team (Bravo) were killed in an ambush we were sucked into. We had good intelligence about a village near our objective that was clear and friendly. Our CIA-provided guide took us in about 0300 hours and something didn't seem right but 'Company' seemed to think everything was fine.

It was. Until we heard the report of an AK-47 and the soldier standing next to me grabbed his chest and went down. We all dropped and looked for shelter. I looked in his eyes and he was gone. We had a 30 minute firefight and we dispatched 15 guerillas and our 'guide'—'Company' took him out with a bullet to the head. I got the impression that 'Company' didn't need his help anymore.

But, we lost three men. We cleaned them up and noted the position of where we buried them and exited the village. After a few hours, no one else came after us so we assumed that we got them all and they had no radio. We moved to our objective and completed our mission. It took two days to get to Cazombo by the truck we appropriated. 'Appropriated' is a word that we sometimes use for stole. We arrived with seven men.

Alpha Team had about the same experience. The started with eleven and ended with six. They had a rather intense firefight at their objective and the government reserves got there very quickly. Their 'Company' Man was KIA (killed in action). The six of them arrived in a jeep a day after us. So, the 13 of us were stuck in a small village with a very scared population. They really didn't know what to make of us and didn't know what we were going to do with them.

While we waited, a very troubling (at the time) thing happened, the village elder, Abu, invited us to a feast. Now, for the confused, I found out later that, in this particular part of Angola, the people referred to their village elder as Abu, or father. Anyway, we went to the feast and they had a wonderful meal displayed. There were vegetables we had seen them collecting and there was meat. The problem was they had no livestock. Or, at least, we had seen nothing . . . not even a lamb.

As we sat down to eat, I looked at 'Tennessee' and gestured to the meat with a questioning glance. He mouthed 'dog' and I shook my head and shifted my eyes so he could see the three dogs we had seen earlier were there. At least we knew we weren't eating dog.

'Street' saw we were concerned and moved his hand at his waist. We looked around and saw none of the children. Our eyes got a little larger. We were knocked out of our reservations by 'Grunt' greeting Ummi.

Ummi and several of the young women of the village brought in drinks and sat them down in front of us. 'Grunt' said thank you in French and told everyone, with no doubt in his voice, to eat.

Our reservations were based on the fact that there were only about 40 adults and adolescents in the village and maybe 20 kids. We had all of the adults over 20 with us. The others were either cooking, serving or outside watching. The kids, we could not see. I mean, we could not see them . . . . anywhere.

We ate our meal. You need to understand, we had no choice. If we had refused to eat the food these people made for us, we could have been killed in our sleep or they would have turned us in to the government or guerillas. We needed to let them know that we trusted them and knew and respected their situation by helping us. When we finished our meal, we went to bed.

In the morning, 'Cat' came in to our shanty laughing. He said, 'come outside'. He showed us the children playing at the end of the street and we saw a couple older women laughing at us.

'Cat' had asked one of them what meat we had eaten the night before and they responded with a quizzical look. Then they saw his eyes open as he saw the kids. They started laughing and pointed to a large building and told him that their custom is to have the children eat separately during ceremonies. I still do not know what we ate. We did not ask again and they never told us.

Charlie Team arrived three days later. Or, at least what was left of them. They started with twelve men. Only four arrived at our location. They had a vicious firefight at a 'secure' location, just as we did. Two men were killed when they were ambushed. They accomplished their objective but were ambushed when trying to evacuate to the rally point.

They were encircled and two men were killed and four captured by the MPLA. Those four were later executed as mercenaries. The executions were carried out on TV. It almost created a diplomatic incident as the government claimed they were American soldiers but they had no proof. The U.S. Secretary of State stated that he knew nothing of them and he was right. This was a CIA and DOD operation. The State Department and the President knew nothing of it. As a matter of fact, the last person we wanted involved was Jimmy Carter or anyone in his administration. Up until recently, those guys were the biggest threat this country faced.

The remaining four arrived in Cazombo tired and wounded. 'Company' made the call to arrange pick up for 17 men.

We would have to wait three more days. Not a big problem. The people were nice, the food was good and the place was relatively peaceful.

---

# 9—Village Rape

It was a relaxing morning. Those of us who were 'healthy' were out stretching. The others were recuperating. Then all hell broke lose.

A kid came running up to Abu and he sent the kid to tell 'Company' something. There was panic on the kid's face but Abu and 'Company' just displayed a sense of urgency.

'Company' came to us and told us to get everyone up and out of the village. He indicated that the boy would show us a safe place. So we grabbed our stuff and our compatriots. We followed the boy a little south of the village and settled down into a defensive position.

We had a few women with us and many of the younger children. Ummi was very concerned but seemed to show that she had been through this many times.

Well, what was happening was the village was being attacked and figuratively raped by the government forces in the area. They were taking anything and anyone they wanted.

In our position, we could not hear much. It was not loud and there were no gunshots. However, we did not see what was to happen.

Abu was being slapped around and the Army Commander was asking him where the rest of the villagers were. He was specifically looking for the young males and the attractive females. The absence of attractive females upset the government soldiers ransacking the huts. The young males being absent seem to indicate that they had gone to join the guerrillas. This infuriated the Commander.

Abu told him that the young men did go with the guerrillas, but they were abducted and forced to be 'soldiers' by another base commander. The Commander wasn't buying it—although it was true—and slapped Abu around a bit more. After getting the same answer from villagers pleading for the life of Abu, he then asked about the women.

The Commander and his soldiers were looking for relaxation. Their form of relaxation is going into a village and taking a few of the young women back to their base to be raped and kept until they were no longer pleasing. This is not exclusive to the military. The guerrillas did the same. Women had very little value to these groups—except to be raped.

The women might be forced to service the soldiers/guerrillas for a few hours to months. If and when they finish with them, if they let them live, they release them and the women have three choices.

The women can walk back to their village where everyone will accept them but everyone will also know that they had been violated. Any child born of the rapes would be considered a second-class citizen in the village.

Or, the women can go to another village and make up a story about their husband being killed or taken by either the military or the guerrillas. In this case, the woman would be accepted, although the villagers will suspect that she had been raped. Any child would be accepted but with a little doubt in everyone's mind.

The last acceptable choice for the women is to commit suicide. Unfortunately, this is the choice that most women took.

Other than dying during the rape marathon, the remaining possibility for the woman—in many cases just a girl—was that the men would keep her so long in their camp that she would become an asset that they might keep around or trade to other units.

Eventually, she lost all hope of escape and became a zombie in the rape bed of the camp.

Abu told the Commander that the guerrillas took all the females, even his two little daughters. The Commander seemed placated. But, there still had to be someone they could use. There was. One of the villagers had been down near the Zambeze River and did not know the soldiers were raiding. She returned at the wrong time.

When the soldiers brought the 15 year-old girl to the Commander, he asked her why the guerrillas did not take her. She told him that she had been hiding. The Commander laughed and said, "Not good enough. Put her in my jeep."

The girl started screaming and the soldiers dragged her away. Abu could only beg and the other villagers pleaded. All to no avail.

The Commander yelled to them, "We will take good care of her to protect her from the guerrillas." And, they drove away.

All of the above was told to us by Abu as he was being treated for his beating. 'Company' told us that this happened often to all the villages. There were beatings, rapes and killings on a regular basis all over Angola.

Many of the guerrillas were young boys who had been kidnapped and indoctrinated or coerced into fighting. After a while, the boys grow up to accept and belong. They accept the behavior as justified and they belong to the guerrillas. Leaving is not an option except by death.

The government did not 'take' the young men. They did their best to 'convince' the young males that it would be better to volunteer to be in the Army. This convincing was done while the boys were being held in jail until the local commander was sure they were not a guerrilla. Many times, the boys were told that if they did not join the Army that their family might suffer death—from the guerrillas. The boys knew that the Army would return to their village and kill their family. They joined.

Because of all this, the typical village was filled with very young children; boys under the age of 12 were visible. The females were also very young or very old. The only adolescents you would see were cripples or those who showed the raiders that they had a venereal disease.

At least for now, the village felt they were safe. The guerillas were not in the area because the military was. The soldiers would not return as they usually came about 2-3 times a month. Abu felt that they would have a week of peace. He was wrong.

I don't know if they tortured the girl they took or if the Commander just knew Abu was lying. But, they knew there were other females in the village. And, they knew when to raid—dinner time. What the soldiers did not anticipate was an armed force in the village.

The soldiers swooped down on the village like vultures just as the women were preparing dinner. We all reacted as we heard the jeeps approaching quickly from both ends of the village. We hid in the huts we were using and Abu had gathered all the villagers behind him in the village center.

The Commander slapped Abu for lying to him. When another man tried to intercede, the Commander shot him. At this time, we were all locking and loading. 'Company' motioned for us to relax and indicated he believed there would be little trouble. What he didn't see was that the soldiers had already started searching all the huts. Eventually, they would find us. But, that wasn't the match that started the bonfire.

Out in the village center, the Commander had told his soldiers to take Ummi. She was older—about 35—but they would use her to punish Abu. Then he asked Abu, "Are these your daughters?" He was pointing at the two little girls holding on to Ummi. "I thought you said they were dead." Then he told his soldiers to hold the toddlers about ten feet away. "I will make your words a reality." He then pulled a machete out of his jeep. That's what started the fight.

'Company' and Lt. Ball were the first two out of the hut. The rest of us followed. It seemed as though the other groups all had the same idea as all 3 huts emptied of 17 men, armed and ready to defend these people. There was no way that monster was going to touch those little girls.

'Tennessee' was the one who put a bullet between the Commander's eyes. Just as he was raising the machete to kill Xhosa, 'Tennessee' exited the hut behind the girls and killed the butcher. A battle ensued and the villagers hit the dirt and scrambled to cover.

I will admit that many of the soldiers fought well, but we had taken them by surprise and they had come with a lackadaisical attitude of dealing with old people and children. Within five minutes, 20 soldiers were dead or wounded. Abu told his villagers to make sure the soldiers were dead and we heard some screams of wounded men being killed. As professional soldiers, this should have bothered us, but these men were not soldiers. They were rapists, kidnappers and murderers. Their primary tool was terror. We had no compassion for those 'executed' by their intended victims.

While the cleaning up was being done by the 'old men and women,' the older children were packing belongings in their huts. 'Company' and Abu were talking. I wasn't sure what was going on, but I knew the villagers weren't staying and neither were we. I assumed we were leaving together.

Lt Ball told us to 'saddle up' and told us we would be camping out a couple days. There was a potential LZ (landing zone) near Macondo but we had to avoid the government troops that would be looking for us in about an hour. 'Company' came up and told us that we would have 14 of the villagers accompanying us. These were Abu's family members. It seems that half of the village was related to him and the other half had come from another village only recently.

'Company' hooked up the radio as we prepared the jeeps the government has now so graciously donated to our cause. He told his people that we would need a CH-47 Chinook as we would have up to 31 people and he would explain later. There didn't seem to be any argument. I guess they were either very flexible or they knew he had control of their actions.

Ball decided that we would take all of the vehicles that entered the village that morning. We gave our previously appropriated vehicles to the remaining villagers who headed towards Lusaka, Zambia. If they had been found later with the vehicles from today, they would be slaughtered. We would be killed anyway so we took all the chances. We headed out. The other group headed towards Lusaka. 'Company' and Abu determined that it would be the safest large city and they could find their friends later.

The village, the soldiers' bodies and the remaining government vehicles where set on fire and left to burn. Everything that could identify the bodies was taken and their faces and any other feature had been obliterated by the villagers. We loaded up the jeeps and one truck and hit the road. We hoped that we would have 3-4 hours but figured we had one hour.

---

# 10—Escape

It didn't take long and we hit the road. The three jeeps and the truck were loaded with 'refugees', soldiers and a few select belongings. The children were crying because everyone was hurrying and telling them nothing. The women were upset because they had to leave their homes and loved ones they knew they would never see alive again. The men were stoic but I knew they were scared for their families.

'Company' received a call and was told that Zambia was not 'officially' giving any U.S. Government aircraft permission to land in their country. This endangered our pickup chances north of Mankoya. The Rhodesian military has offered to come in and get us but we would need to get as close to their border as possible. They would like us to get near Mulobezi.

We had a one hour head start and 300 miles to go. The CH47 would be there in 14 hours. It wasn't going to be easy.

The government troops took about an hour to decide that their commander was late getting back. They made jokes about him enjoying himself too much in the small village and tasting too many of the morsels—raping the girls. But, the pre-determined time had expired and they did go looking for him. Thankfully, they were taking their time and it took about another hour for them to be ready. We had a two-and-a-half hour head start when we expected one.

Of course, the soldiers entered the village loaded for bear and immediately saw that there had been a firefight. They weren't sure what happened but they were sure their side lost. There were bodies staked under debris left from huts the bodies died in. they dug through and discovered the bodies were their soldiers and their commander's body was in the central hut. He had been decapitated but he was identified by his right foot missing two twos. This was something no one had noticed as they took his boots but not his socks.

The Army had a problem. The first thing they had to do was determine what happened and which way to pursue. Was it the guerrillas and do they chase them into the jungle and get ambushed? Or, was it the villages and do they head off down the road and try to catch and butcher them? But, which way? There are three roads and they entered from one of them.

We did take the time to make it look as though the guerrillas had attacked or had been helping the villagers. Unfortunately, we had to make a couple of the dead villagers look as though they were guerrillas. Their families did not like it, but Abu explained and they understood. The sub-commander was concerned but didn't want it to be guerrillas.

It took the officer in charge a short while to realize that there were two sets of tracks out of the village—South and East-southeast. But, he needed permission and more troops. He was not going to act on his own. This was the first break we got.

Two hours allotted for the commander to enjoy himself, minus thirty minute travel time. One hour delay before they realized there might be something wrong. The additional hour and a half to get ready. Thirty minutes to travel and thirty minutes to decide what to do. Two hours to get permission and troops. They took seven hours to begin their pursuit. We were in luck.

The weather was good. The roads were dry. The villagers cooperated in everything. By the time the soldiers began chasing us, we were nearing Makoya. We were home free.

Twelve hours later, we arrived at the designated pick-up point and 'Company' gave the call. Now, all we had to do was wait.

Abu's brother (Jimoh) decided he wanted to stay. This took us by surprise. We thought that everyone who was with us would be staying with us. Anyone who left would not only be vulnerable but would put us at risk if they were captured.

But his wife had been raped and killed by the guerrillas in front of him and their village. His son had been taken by the guerrillas when he was nine—two years ago. His daughter Anana (soft, gentle) had been taken last year by government forces for their pleasure rooms—she was 13. Jimoh (born on Friday) wanted to find his daughter and take her to Lusaka with their other villagers.

Everyone else was happy to escape. We didn't hear about the others. The chopper arrived and 30 people climbed on board. We disabled the vehicles and made sure that no evidence of our being there was left.

Three days later, I was back in the states sitting at home. I had told my wife that we were deployed in Georgia for training. 'Tennessee' told the same to his wife and that's the way it was. I can only assume that the soldiers who did not return alive 'died in a training accident'. I never saw any of them until I saw 'Cat' in Germany in '85. That's when I learned his real name.

The villagers arrived covertly at Fort Gordon, GA a week later. They had refugee papers and were granted dual citizenship. They were given time to acclimate and learn the language. They were taught trades. After about six months, they went on with their lives with generous support from the government to buy homes and cars. Often I wondered about them but I didn't see or hear of any of them again.

But . . . . back to the present.

---

# 11—AIDS Cure Discovered

We arrived in D.C. and went to the Pentagon. I couldn't help but notice the repaired wall and cursed Carter and Clinton under my breath. The two men responsible for 9/11 and the 'lamestream' media blames "W". Screw 'em. Line up all reporters and lawyers and shoot them.

We went through the various levels of security and down several long halls. When we went in a small conference room, I saw three non-military personnel and a few support personnel milling around. I was introduced to LAPD Detective Lt. Johnson, Dr. Rodriguez from the USC Medical Center, and ICE Agent Mark Testerman. The presence of these people and their jobs didn't make anything any clearer.

LTG Ball told all the support people to leave and asked everyone to take their seats. His first words were, "Gentlemen, this is Sergeant Major Raymond. He retired 15 years ago and is the sole remaining member of 'Operation Hackman'. He remembers the operation and some of the people involved."

"I have not told him anything else. That is left up to you three. You each have details and maybe together we can come up with a complete picture. Doctor, you might want to begin."

Dr. Rodriguez began, "I will be blunt. Sergeant Major, we have found a cure for AIDS and we need you to secure it."

Of course, I sat up straight and replied, "What? This is amazing. How could this secret be kept? How am I involved? How long have you known about this and where is it?"

The doctor responded, "We have found a person whose blood is immune to HIV and has destroyed the AIDS infection and all other STDs and **any** disease introduced to it. I understand you have a medical background so you understand blood tests. Suffice it to say that THE CURE has been found. You seem to be the only person connected with the donor of the blood. We need your help."

"Doctor, I am fascinated by all this," I said. "How was this discovery made? Who is involved that I know and what is the progress on replicating the blood cells?"

"All good questions. We made the discovery by doing a routine blood test on an Los Angeles prostitute. You do know—or did know the lady—she is now deceased. And, unfortunately, by the time we started the routine post-mortem tests, her body had been cremated as a homeless indigent. Who was she? I'll let Lieutenant Johnson take over."

The detective began, "Do you remember . . . I guess she would have been a little girl then. Do you remember Mandisa?"

I took a few seconds to think through 50-plus years of names and visualized the two little girls and replied that I did. I visualized a sweet little girl playing in the village center with her sister.

He continued and took about five minutes to tell me his knowledge of her activities in LA and her death.

When he finished, I stated, "Well, all of this is fantastic but I still do not get my connection."

Agent Testerman spoke up, "That's where I come in. After they did their investigation and came up with nothing, I was contacted by these gentlemen and I understood why they wanted to keep only a few people involved. If this possible 'cure' is announced, there would be pandemonium. My understanding is that only the people in this room know what you have just heard. I understood right away why no one else in my office could help me and when the DOD got involved, my superiors gave me a free reign. Let me fill you in."

I was a little shocked. "How could those glamour hogs in Obama's White House not announce they had cured AIDS? I cannot believe anyone there knows what we are doing."

Ball offered, "Sergeant Major, the current 'commander-in chief' (said with an eye roll) has too many important issues, like apologizing to the world for the U.S.A., to be involved. Suffice it to say that the Secretary of Defense, personally, has given me full control of this mission. The highest career officer in the CIA and ICE are also involved and have given their full cooperation. We all have the same level of 'respect' for the president's priorities. Testerman."

Testerman continued, "Thank you General. When I was first asked about Mandisa, I could find almost nothing in our records. That was very surprising and the first red flag. Then I discovered that she was issued a passport and dual citizenship through our Atlanta office. This was pretty normal but they had no paperwork on file—a second red flag was raised. And, there was no record of her or any family members entering the U.S.A. at any of our legal Ports of Entry. This was a huge red flag. My only conclusions was it had to be a situation that involved the DOD."

I nodded that I understood and Testerman continued, "I contacted an old friend who works here and who worked with Special Ops years ago and I later found out he knew some of your old friends. He told me he would get back with me. A week later, I had a CIA Analyst in my office—asking me questions. When DOD contacts the CIA and they interview ICE, something bigger than me is going on. I was given access to records and was made fully aware of the sensitive nature of events that happened then and are happening now."

"It seems that Mandisa was brought to the U.S.A. in a group of people who were brought from somewhere in Africa—now I know it was Angola—as political refugees. That is all anyone knows. A retired and now deceased CIA operative by the name 'Jenkins' made a detailed report of "Operation Hackman" but the CIA will only release the names of the military operatives in that action but would not release the objective or any other information."

I interjected, "Sir, why is it that every CIA Agent is named 'Jenkins'? I knew Agent Fuhrman by his real name and I know what happened. Everything that is in the record or not in the record is all that is available officially. If my superiors or Fuhrman's decided not to have items included, that was their call. I still cannot legally fill in the details of the operation. If you brought me here for that, . . . . "

"No, Sergeant Major, we don't need the details, we need you. Actually, we need you and/or the general." He looked at LTG Ball and the general made no notice of the comments. "You see, we do know that he was also in the operation although he has repeatedly said you are the sole survivor."

"Here's the situation. We have found all the details we need about the families that came here. We know where they went and what happened to them. The unfortunate thing is that Mandisa was the last remaining live one in the U.S. We need her relatives. Rather, we need to go to Zambia, Angola or Zimbabwe to find her relatives."

"You may recall that her uncle remained in Zambia for some reason . . . ."

I offered, "He wanted to find his daughter and free her and hoped to find his son."

"Well, we've found who we believe is him and where he lives. What you could not have known is that he did locate his daughter. We have heard nothing of a son until you mentioned it. We may have to look into that. Also, it appears that Xhosa Jones and another of the original refugee girls returned to Zambia. We need to go talk with Jimoh and Anana and locate Xhosa. If we find the other girl and she is related, okay. But, right now, she is not a priority. Jimoh, Anana and Xhosa are our objectives."

"Well," I said, "as far as I know, Abu, Ummi, Xhosa and Mandisa were the only family members in our group. I believe Jimoh was Abu's brother but there is nothing certain about that. The other ten were from the village but not related—as far as I know. Of course, the possibility of a bloodline is very possible. But, my understanding is that the village was almost a mini-refugee camp of many small villages throughout Western Angola. They survived their villages' attacks and escaped to the border region. All they wanted was to live free and raise their families."

Agent Testerman continued, "Yes, your knowledge appears to coincide with what we found out. What we did learn had to be done very quietly. Many questions could not be asked to maintain the secrecy. Going through official government channels is out of the question. So, we need to meet and talk with the targets and bring those people here for testing."

"All right, where do I come in?" I asked, "This is a simple visa issue and you bring them here. But, could you please stop calling them 'targets'?"

"It is not really a simple visa issue." LTG Ball chimed in. "Jimoh will only deal with members of the group that saved his family and others. He does not trust any government and very few people. But, he will talk to US and he will help ONLY US—you and me—find the rest of the family. Sergeant Major, we are, as Testerman pointed out, the only two members left of the seventeen who left Zambia that day."

He continued, "So, you see why we needed you. We are going to a region that is still a little unstable. Expect anything and take nothing at face value. We will depart in a two days for Lusaka, Zambia. We will hook up with Jimoh and track down his daughter and any other family members they may know about. We will bring them back to Lusaka and they will be issued visas and will come with us back to Atlanta. The Director of the CDC has been involved since this 'cure' became a possibility and Dr. Rodriguez will lead a team to develop the cure. Any questions?"

I replied, "Yes sir, does Jimoh know why we are looking for him? Is he willing to help us? And, does he agree to come to the U.S.A.?"

"Good questions. Not really, yes and yes. We have not told him that Mandisa is dead. Actually, we have told him that she is very ill and we need him, Anana and Xhosa to get blood to help treat an illness she has and others might have. For that, he is willing to come here. Also, he is ready to leave all the problems of Africa behind."

"If you have no other questions? Anyone? We will have a mission briefing tomorrow and leave tomorrow night. (Aside to his aide) Captain, see that the Sergeant Major gets settled in the hotel and anything else he needs. (To me.) Sergeant Major, I'll see you at oh-nine-hundred tomorrow."

"Yes, sir." We left.

---

# 12—Back to Africa

The flight over was uneventful. Unfortunately, we could not take a military flight from D.C. to Pretoria. It was atypical large airliner and we had to endure first class accommodations as they were all we could get at the last minute. We had attractive air hostesses catering to our every whim. However, we could not talk or discuss anything about what we had to do or expect. All kidding aside, it was a good flight. But, we had a slightly more private plane heading to Lusaka. The CIA had a contact who chartered us a plane.

"General, who is our contact? Who is helping us find the girl?" I asked.

"Xhosa is reported to have returned to Zambia. That is a dead end. But, in Lusaka, we are looking for folks who know how to contact Jimoh, Abu's brother, and his daughter Anana. She was taken to Angola and is a slim-to-none chance for us."

I asked, "What about Jimoh? I do remember but and I think looking for a refugee in a large city after 20 years is a little daunting."

"Well, there's the beauty of it," Ball stated, "he came forward. He came to our Consulate and asked how he could contact his relatives in the U.S.A. He had names and details and the fact that they left with a U.S. Military Special Forces Group. All of this information took a few people by surprise and raised a few eyebrows. It was because of this report being forwarded to Langley that we got our biggest break."

"Did the Consulate help him?"

"Not really. The Consul didn't believe him and didn't care what he said but a senior NCO at the scene told the Consul's career assistant—the local CIA operative—that this should be investigated as it is possible he's telling the truth. The Gunny took his information and asked him to keep in touch as they looked. He has been back a few times over the last two years so they know him and he knows we are trying to help him. But, he has now stated that he will only talk with us."

"It looks like fate is on our side," I said. "Looks like we are landing."

---

# 13—Lusaka Meeting

We arrived at the Consulate and LTG Ball and I were met as dignitaries. We were led immediately to the Consul's office and waited a few minutes. The whole time, the general was putting on airs of agitation.

"General, something doesn't seem right." I began. "If they knew we were coming and we needed to talk with Jimoh, why do I get the feeling something is wrong?"

"Sergeant Major, I haven't been completely honest with you. Jimoh has come here often, but not in the last six months. His 'nephew' has come and he says Jimoh has gone home. We're not sure what that means. The only thing we know now is that the Consul has information and needs to talk with us."

The Consul enters the room with his assistant who is obviously a CIA operative and his very attractive secretary. Democrat appointees always seem to have attractive secretaries.

"Good morning, Mr. Ball, Mr. Raymond, glad to see you arrived in perfect spirits." the Consul started.

I looked at the General and he nodded toward the assistant. I looked at him and he slightly shook his head 'no'. The Consul did not know we were military and had absolutely no idea of our mission.

The Consul continued, "Since the President (nodding toward Obama's picture) appointed me, I have felt like a fish out of water. It is nice to see some non-uniform guys visit me. The Marines here and the local hires are all stupid and I replaced anyone I could. Even my assistant, Mr. Jenkins, is new as I discovered his predecessor was a CIA agent and could not have him not in our—the President's and my—camp. That said, why did 'our' president send you?"

It was all I could do to not laugh and biting my tongue helped. This guy was about as liberal with a capital L as they come . . . and about as naïve. He really did not know they replaced one agent with another. Hell, I was pretty sure his 'hot' secretary got her typing skills at Langley also.

The General began, "Mr. Consul, the president wants to establish a few 'special' agreements with some of the local government leaders. Over the past two years, an agent from Zimbabwe, a Mr. Jimoh, has been establishing a presence here and is our contact. He has been our contact with some very, shall we say, generous contacts who understand how two 'progressive' governments can work together. However, some people have gotten wind of the scheduled meeting and Mr. Jimoh had to stop his visits."

The Consul nodded and replied, "Yes. When I got here, I was told that Jimoh was looking for his family in the U.S.A. I was not really interested. But, when Mr. Jenkins arrived, I was told of the 'real' nature of Jimoh's business."

Mr. Jenkins added, "Sir, if I might." He paused for approval to continue. "Jimoh has been our contact with several local governments for several years. It was President Mugabe who set up this system when President Clinton was in office. Under Bush, little actions was taken as there was no interest in aligning with the countries in question. Now, thanks to having 'our' man in office, we can meet with people who see our vision of the world. Mr. Jimoh is the key. But, he will only meet with Mr. Raymond." He looked at me.

The General grabbed my leg under the table and I knew I had to act like I knew what was going on. "Yes," I said, "it appears that we have a mutual friend from Libya."

General Ball smiled and Jenkins continued—ad lib, " . . . Right. He will talk with us but he is concerned about all the people who have left, many of whom were aligned with our beliefs." He looked at the Consul who shrugged. "And, it seems that he does not trust the people here any longer."

LTG Ball was a master of politics and changing operations on the go. He took the Company man's lead and took charge of the meeting.

Ball asked, "So, where do we stand? Did we come all this way for nothing because someone was a little overzealous in his purge?" He looked at the Consul.

The Consul began, "See here, I was appointed by the president . . . ."

Ball cut him off, "Yes, to make things easier not ruin everything! I am sure Mr. Obama will be happy to hear of your destroying years of work toward his dreams of one world order. Upon my return, I will be glad to tell him anything you wish me to say on your behalf. Or, you can shut-up and let the real professionals do their jobs."

The Consul had nothing to say in his defense and had never been yelled at in his life. "I will let Mr. Jenkins take over from here. It seems that Mr. Jimoh's agent will only deal with him now." He rose to leave.

Jenkins nodded toward the door and said, "We can use my office." He then looked at the Consul's secretary and told her, "We won't be needing you any longer." She looked at the Consul, who had stopped at his office door, and he shrugged.

We headed down the hall and passed Jenkins' office. We continued into the Marine Embassy Guard Barracks area. He nodded to the gunnery sergeant outside a door who opened it for us and entered. Two armed marines took their posts outside the door. It was beginning to look more like old times.

Jenkins looked at the Gunnery Sergeant and made introductions. "Gunny, this is Lieutenant General Ball and Sergeant Major Raymond. They are your charges now."

Gunny replied, "Yes, sir. Coffee gentlemen? I am sure you were offered tea upstairs, but here we like a cup of Joe." We nodded and he got us coffee and placed a map on the table.

Jenkins began, "General, we have a problem. It seems that idiot upstairs appointed by our Socialist-in-Chief has made our contact disappear. We have been looking for him and we discovered he did leave Lusaka."

Ball broke in, "Do we have any idea where he is?"

Jenkins replied, "Yes, sir, we have an idea and some leads. Thankfully, Gunny has been here a few years and has friends in the city. But, General, I have to ask, why did you guys come all this way to talk to him? I mean, I am given this whole story and told to develop a cover story and help your guys. What is going on?"

"Agent Jenkins," Ball replied, "if the Agency did not tell you what is going on, then they did not want you to know. It has nothing to do with trust. The Sergeant Major and I are trusting you and Gunny with our lives. But, we cannot tell you the importance of this man. If Langley decides to tell you what is going on, so be it. We are here as representatives of key agencies in the U.S. Government and you can rest assured, I will NOT be talking with Obama anytime soon."

Jenkins replied, "I understand and I am emboldened by your last assurance. Let's go find Jimoh."

We drank a few cups of coffee and talked about some adventures. After a few hours, Jenkins called the consul's secretary and told him we would be leaving out the side door. She is his sister and does work for the CIA.

The secretary told the consul she was informed by her contact that we were leaving. A big show of pompousness was made in our departure as we left the building and got in our limo to go back to our hotel. We had to make sure he thought we had Obama's ear. That was her job and she did it well.

---

# 14—The Search for Jimoh—Angola

Angola is much the same now as in 1978, except when I left people were trying to kill me. When I found out we were returning, I had to find out why. Now, that said, I have been to many places where people tried to kill me and I have returned to visit and have great vacations.

I asked, "Jenkins, two questions. First, why is every agent I meet named Jenkins. And, second, why are we looking here rather than Zambia?"

He chuckled and replied, "A long time ago we had an agent who used the name Jenkins who was very successful and very lucky. One might say he was almost bulletproof. In his career he was dispatched to about 20 countries and had been involved in dozens of firefights. He had never been shot or even scratched. Someone decided it was a lucky name. But, for a more serious issue . . . . It has come to our attention that Anana has been found and knows where her father is and is willing to talk . . . . if we help her."

"Help her? What sort of trouble is she in? Why is it that this does not sound good?" I asked.

"Well, as you know, Anana was taken at the age of 13 by the soldiers. After one year or so, and after she had been raped a thousand times, she was released. After many years, her father found her but he was unable to get her free. He needed our help and we were unable to help her because of the jerk in the Consulate. But now, thanks to our new carte blanche, we are now able to do anything to help her and Jimoh and maybe whatever your mission is."

I asked, "Where is she that he could not 'free' her? Are we going back into combat? I haven't fired a shot since '92."

"Don't worry Sergeant Major," Jenkins said, "we have plenty of guns and I am sure you know it all comes back to you . . . . Oh, we're near the border, here's your new passports. I took the initiative to believe you guys did not want to be identified as there seems to be something really interesting about your mission."

Ball took his and opened it. "I finally visited Australia! I always wanted to go there." We laughed. "I am George H. Walker? Do I work in the jungle? Or the Bush" We all laughed again. He muttered, "George of the Jungle." I don't think he noticed the George Herbert Walker Bush possibility.

Mine was also perfect, old picture and everything. Even my last trip to Japan in '09 was there. Everything seemed the same except my name—Thomas G. Swinson.

We were preparing to enter Angola at Chicote via Road 320. It should be an easy deal as there are no wars and we have no guns and, most importantly, we do have money.

When we stopped, the officer in charge recognizes that we are four 'Americans' then realizes we are two Americans and two Australians. Three of us have short hair. Gunny's high-and-tight is pretty easy to belief he is a military man but in Australia it is also a proper style. The captain motions us inside.

The Captain stands behind a counter and we all stand abreast as he looks at our passports. He looks over my shoulder and I hear the two guards behind us exit. He asks, "Where are you traveling today, Mr. Walker?" While looking at Ball.

"We are going to Coutada Publica do Longa Mavinga to go on a photo safari." Jenkins offers.

The captain looks at him and replies, "You are photographers but I did not see any camera equipment. Why are you coming from Zambia when you could have arrived in Luando."

Jenkins replied, "Luando is a lot farther away. We are not carrying our equipment because along Road 320, there are many people who might rob you. Not everyone is as honest as you and your soldiers, captain." At this, he had his wallet out and a hand full of twenties exposed. "We are very concerned about our loss. What would you estimate are the odds of our being robbed?"

The captain smiled and replied, "I would say it is one hundred to one." Jenkins gave him $400.

The captain smiles, stamps our passports and motions to the door. "Have a great photo safari in my great country."

Gunny gets back behind the wheel and we drive off. He asks, "Where to sir?"

Jenkins replies, "Muncondo." He sees our puzzled looks. "Anana is there. Jimoh's agent told us where to find her and gave us a recent picture. We are going to get her out of an indentured servant relationship."

I lay my head back and went to sleep. This was going to be an interesting trip. The first man I killed was in this country, I hope the last won't be.

About three hours later, we reached Cunjamba. It is the last small town on the road before having to four-wheel it into the mountains to Muncondo. We stopped outside a little café and went inside. As we entered, six other whites got to their feet and greeted Jenkins and Gunny. They all had long hair and the look that they were either Company men, Delta or SF. I began to think the fun is about to begin.

"Gentlemen, be seated, we will dispense with introductions and have a drink before we leave." Jenkins said. He motioned to the waitress and asked for four cokes and another of whatever the men are drinking.

While we were taking our time to drink a seven ounce coca-cola, two of the men left. I could see out the window that they went to their cars and were moving back and forth between theirs and ours. The 'leader' of their groups said loudly, "Those are the cameras that you men sent ahead for your photo shoot. I hope they are all in good shape. Come, we will take you to the base camp for your safari."

As we were leaving, he tipped the waitress $40 (a week's pay for her) and told the owner, "You never saw us." He gave the man a thick envelope. I am sure the owner had doubled his yearly profits.

I noticed a leather case on my seat and opened it as the general opened his. Inside was two 9MM handguns, loaded, with another six clips in the case. I took off my jacket and put on the dual shoulder holster that was enclosed. I put the pistols in their place and donned my jacket. No words were said, none were needed. Personally, I would have preferred .45s but beggars can't be choosers.

Gunny got into one of the other cars. He seemed to know these guys. The 'leader' took the driver's seat. We were on our way. In about 20 minutes and about 10 miles of four-wheeling up a dry creek bed, we pulled over.

The leader pulled out a map of the area. He laid out the general terrain. And pointed to our destination. By 'our' I mean in our vehicle. The other two vehicles will enter from two other directions as we will triangulate the man's farm. It looked like a small village was nearby with about eight farms around the area. The total population might have been 300.

The leader began, "The farmer bought Anana when she was 16. She has worked there as an indentured servant—really a slave—since 1980. Jimoh has tried to break her out after he tried to buy her freedom. The farmer wants $1000 for her. She's 45 years old and he thinks she is worth $1000! It doesn't smell right to me, but it has been confirmed that this guy traffics in slaves. We do know she wants to leave."

Jenkins broke in, "Do we expect any resistance?"

"We expect that either the slaver will take our $500 offer and let us leave, or try to ambush us on-site and take the money, or let us leave with her and ambush us on the way out. Two things are certain. He is going to try to take our money. And, we are not getting out of there with her without killing someone. So, we are going in locked-and—loaded."

"We will use a modified version of a Zulu tactic. We will be team one and we are going in the front—the bull's head. Teams two and three will go around the perimeter and will drop off three men half way and the other three will come in from the top in their vehicles when the shooting starts. That is sixteen of us to our estimated 20 potential fighters he has. We do not know exactly how many slaves he has and be aware that some of the slaves may fight for him. We are going after one person, no one else. Kill anyone with a gun. The slaves can fend for themselves after we leave. The locals will assume it was a slave-owner dispute."

As we were driving up to the front of the main house, we could see that there were armed men on either side in sheds. We parked and exited the vehicle. The owner came out and he had an older woman behind him. It was Anana. For a 45-year-old with 32 years in slavery, she looked pretty good. If nothing else, finding her was easy.

Jenkins began talking with the owner and they were discussing the need for someone who could speak a dialect in Cabango and that we heard he had an older woman there who comes from the area. Anana raised her head and looked at us. She may have realized what was happening and turned to go inside. The owner asked her where she was going and she stopped.

He walked over to her and spun her around. He stated, "Many people have asked about her in the last two years, even her father–an old man who wanted to take her home before he died. But, he looked very healthy and she is an old army whore. Look at how young and good she looks. Why did he want her? Another came and wanted to buy her last month. Now, you come and need her? Why does everyone need this old whore? She is worthless, even now, I only use her once a month as I have many young girls to use. She has two daughters so she is fertile."

Anana put her head down in shame. He continued, "But, I am a business man. I will sell her to you for $2000."

Jenkins replied, "I could leave here with ten women half her age for that money or with four young girls. But, I am generous and will offer $250."

The owner laughed, "if you want ten women, I will sell them also. But, she will cost you . . . . $1000 . . . . If you buy another $1000 worth of pleasure."

Jenkins answered, "You are most generous with your 'daughters' as I know you treat all your guests well. But, are we not also guests? I can give you $300 for her because we need her language. And, we will consider one young girl and two women of 20 all for $1000."

At this time, the owner had been waving around with his right hand and holding his left hand near his waist. Also, we noted that two of his guards had moved up on either side at 90 degrees and there were at least two others behind us.

The owner took over the deal, "$300 for her language? For $300, I can cut off her head and give it to you. But, if you want her to speak, it will be $700 for her and $800 for one girl and two women I pick. Do you want her daughters?"

Jenkins could tell that it was going nowhere fast. He nodded yes. He turned to 'leader' and asked for his case. While taking the case, he moved his eyes to let me and the general know to take the men behind us. The leader and Jenkins would take the side men. Nothing was said and all was understood.

Jenkins took the case and placed it on a small table in front of the slave owner. He said, we have a deal, $1500 for the old one, two aged 20 and one young girl. I will show you the money and we will trade when your daughters are brought to us."

The owner raised his left hand and put his right behind his back. He yelled to his men, "We have a deal. Take care of our guests."

At this, Jenkins pulled out a gun and shot the owner in the chest. He turned and shot the man to our left. 'Leader' took out the man to the right and the general and I shot the two behind us.

Women and girls started running everywhere out of the sheds and six men ran out with guns. Our vehicle was taking hits. But, thankfully, these guys have the same marksmanship skills as LA gangstas. They fired about 200 rounds and hit our jeep 5 or 6 times. We fired a collective 15 rounds and 11 men lay dead.

At the same time, the six men pinching in on our triangle killed the other 12 men who were either patrolling or guarding the 'crops' tending to their food. In all, 23 slavers were killed in about 3 minutes. Does anyone feel bad? Except for one young woman who was laying across one of the guards and sobbing, it looked like the 60-70 women and girls were happy to be free.

Jenkins had corralled Anana and she told him she had to help them escape. He stood back as she started to bark out orders. Some of the older women went to get vehicles and the teens gathered food and clothes out of the buildings. Two 20-somethings were assigned to watch the one 'mourner'. Within 30 minutes, trucks were heading out west toward the road. One or two headed up the trails in other directions. Before leaving, Anana looked at the mourner and one older woman behind her ran her through with a pitchfork as the two others held her. Anana waved to two well-dressed girls and they ran to the jeeps.

Jenkins said, "Anana, wait, who are they? Are they your daughters? We came for you and did not know of them."

Anana looked him in the eyes and said, "Yes, they are my daughters 11 and 13. Either we all come with you or I go with them. You decide."

We had little choice. The girls climbed in one vehicle and Anana got in ours between the general and me. We headed out northeast toward Machumba and Road 296. The border guards there have already been bought and we will cross easily.

We all settled in for a long ride. Anana looked at each of us. She stated, "the driver is too young and so is the buyer (Jenkins). Which one of you is Raven?"

I raised my hand to shake hers and said, "That would be me. I have known your father for many years and knew your Uncle Abu. We are very grateful for your help." What she didn't know was that, if she was a direct relative and had the same blood, we and the whole world would be glad she is alive. It was not time to mention this. From looking at her and her daughters and knowing a little of her history, I suspected she might have the same healing blood.

She answered, "I have heard of you from my father. He told me all of your names but I could only remember a few. I told his friend a few names and he returned last month and told me 'Raven' was coming to save me as you saved my family. And, now you are saving my family."

Jenkins said that we had a long trip and we had a long time to get acquainted. Anana and I talked for several hours. I never bothered telling her that the general was the man she knew as 'Grunt'. He preferred it that way. She did tell us her story.

---

# 15—Anana's Ordeal in Slavery

Along the way, Anana related her memories of her family and village. She remembered her Uncle Abu and the way he ran their home and village. He was a good chieftain. Her Aunt Ummi was like another mother to her. Her cousins Mandisa and Xhosa were like sisters. She remembered when Mandisa arrived and many were happy to welcome here as on the day Xhosa was born. At the time, I didn't put too much on her choice of words—arrived versus born—but later it becomes significant.

She told us of the troubles that started between the guerrillas and government troops and how the villages were only pawns in their rape and killing games. No one really wanted to be in charge as there was nothing to be in charge of. They only wanted to use the weak.

Abu and Jimoh did well to guess when the raiders would come. The young men would go into the jungle and protect and hide the young girls. Each time, the story would be the same, the young people are gone because the other raiders took them. There is no food in the village because the others took the supplies. The old people cannot leave as they have nowhere to go.

Every once in a while, the men would rape an old woman or beat up a village elder. Abu was beaten several times. Aunt Ummi and other women were raped many times in front of the village. This was a way they showed that they were in control. Rarely did anyone get taken as the system worked. No one thought less of the victims as they knew they were sacrificing themselves for their children. Then her world was torn apart.

Everyone's luck runs out and Abu could not always be right. One day the government troops raided Anana's village at one in the morning and took her and several other young women. One of the girls was her cousin Abeni (girl prayed for). After being thrown in the truck, Anana was punched and knocked out. When she awoke, she heard noise and opened her eyes a little and saw that Abeni was being held down.

As one man finished, another replaced him. By Anana's count she was taken by at least 5 men after she revived. She had no idea how many while she was unconscious. During the rape, the truck hit a bump and one of the soldiers got made at Abeni. He was furious and pulled out his knife and slit her throat. Anana did all she could not to scream. The others were all laughing.

They reached the camp. When they lowered the ramp, Abeni's body fell out and the Commander was heard to say that he was glad they already took their share.

Anana and the other three girls in her truck were pulled out and stood in front of the Commander. He walked in front of them and touched them at will and looked into their mouths. He then motioned to Anana and she was taken to his quarters. Then the next senior officer had his choice and the two remaining girls were giving to the NCOs.

The commander raped Anana that night and when he woke in the morning. As he tended to his military duties, she was helped to get clean by an older woman (maybe 30) who Anana later found out was the commander's wife. She bathed, changed into clean clothes and ate. Then she waited in the Commander's bedroom. Whenever he felt he had time, he would enter and she was ordered to strip and he would rape her again. Sometimes, his wife would help. On one occasion, he brought in a new officer to show him how it was done and how easy it was. Anana lost any semblance of shame as she knew it would only get her beaten and would not stop the assaults.

This continued for over a month. Anana was told by the commander's wife that he liked her because she was younger than she was. When she gets too 'used', she will be sent to the subordinate officers and become their property. Then, she will move down to the sergeants and finally to the troops until she dies, gets a disease or they kick her out of camp. In the first two months, she was raped by the Commander at least 100 times.

After another month, a strange incident occurred. The regional Colonel arrived to inspect the camp. Part of his inspections was the use of Anana and the Commander's quarters. The Colonel also had his traveling slave and Anana was expected to put on a good show with her. During the week the Colonel took her maybe 10 times by himself and another 3-4 with his slave and the rest of the time, the two women were required to remain nude. While this sounds bad, it would come back to save her later.

The commander did like Anana, but when new girls came in, still took the best each time and Anana was expected to watch as she was raped by the Commander and in many cases deflowered. The Commander almost always took the youngest woman to ensure he had a virgin. Many times he bragged that he averaged 10 virgins a month. On a few occasions, Anana had to hold the young woman to keep her from fighting. She did this while telling the victim that if she fought, she would die. Anana did not like what she had to do, but she was living and was being raped by only one man at a time.

After three months, Anana was sent out when an a younger victim was brought in. The Commander found a new favorite and Anana would become the property of the Executive Officer. But, he just got a new young woman and didn't want Anana. She just had another birthday and was an 'old woman'. And, she became the property of the junior officers—she moved in with five men and was raped that first day repeatedly.

For the next month, she was raped every day at least once by each of the five. The assaults never seem to stop. She was expected to bathe after each and keep clean for the next 'master' to use her. In four months, she had been raped over hundreds of times. She was ready to die, but wanted to live.

After a year of abuse, her chance came to escape. The military camp was attacked by Banks and his men. They were looking to kill soldiers and destroy everything but the ammunition. With explosions everywhere and all the buildings on fire, Anana and others took to the jungles. Banks' men were not interested in them.

After the destruction, many of the girls were found nearby in the woods by the soldiers. They stayed near because they could not return home after being violated. But, Anana and a few others did escape. When the Commander was looking for an accurate count, he was told that many of the charred bodies in the buildings were unidentifiable. He assumed the women had been killed.

Anana and two girls headed west to Calomo. She did not know that her father's family had gone to Zambia and she did not know he was looking for her. But, the girls knew that if they headed back to their homes, the soldiers would find them.

The three stayed together for a year and traveled as three refugees from village to village, staying each place for a short time and then leaving. They stayed ahead of the raids and got lucky until 1980, Anana was now 16 and the girls with her were similar ages. Their happiness ended in the early morning hours.

They were in a small village near Gime and they were surrounded and raided by guerrillas about 3 AM. The old people who fought were killed, the young men who could fight were executed if they did not die in the fight. The young and teen boys were manacled and put in a truck. The children, girls under 12 and boys under 8, were run off. The women over 30 were mercilessly abused and some died or were killed in the process. The raid lasted over six hours.

The village was suspected of helping the government troops. There would be a lesson today. The village chief watched his wife and nineteen year old daughter being abused while he and his fifteen year old son were tied in chairs where the women could knew they were being forced to watch. When the assault ended. The chief's youngest daughter was held in the air by two guerrillas as the leader stabbed her. The chief's family watched her scream twice and then go into shock and die of her internal bleeding as she was being held. The men threw her body onto the fire.

The leader asked if the chief wanted to tell him anything to save their lives. The chief denied knowing anything but inadvertently looked at one of Anana's companions to the side. The leader took this as a sign and had the girl brought forward. The other friend took off running and was shot by a perimeter guard. A guerilla went to her body and as she lay bleeding. The leader watched as the guerilla shot her in the head. The leader laughed.

Anana's friend screamed that she knew nothing and the chief cried that it was a mistake, he did not look at her. The leader said that if it was a mistake, then she has seen nothing and has nothing to say. He had a guerrilla hold her as he stuck a pin in each eye and while she was screaming he held her tongue and cut it out. He told the one holding her, she is yours. He held her head back by the hair and she chocked to death as he held her. She was thrown on top of the little girl.

But, the leader was not finished. He looked at the village chief and asked who he loved the most, his wife or his son or daughter. The chief could not answer. His wife screamed out that he loved her the most. The leader turned to her and said, 'I believe you and

I will give you love like him but you talk when you are not spoken to.' He had one man cut out her tongue. As she was spitting and choking on blood, the leader moved behind her and began beating her with his cane. She tried to scream and drooped dead over the barrel she was tied to.

The leader then told him that he may remember this lesson but will leave a reminder. He made many slices on the daughter's face and told the chief that every time you look at her, you will remember your wife's love. He then told his men to take the chief's son. They would never see each other again.

Anana and the young girls were taken to the guerrilla camp. She would remain there for two years. In that time, she would be raped thousands of times and would endure many pregnancies and would be beaten until she aborted. They wanted women, not babies.

In 1982, the guerrillas found a new way to make money. They would sell their captives they no longer wanted to local farmers or to slave traders. Anana was sold to her first 'farm' in Talapo. She was 18 and was a true slave to work in the fields. This did not stop the farmer or his slave-driver from using her and the others. She stayed there three years and had a child who died at age one. After her child died, she was sold to a slaver.

It was 1985 and she was sold to a man in Quioco. He was looking for girls he could fatten up and sell in the Congo. For the first time, since 1977, she was actually fed and treated well and examined by a doctor. This man wanted to make sure his stock was healthy. She was 21 and attractive. Once she got some weight on her, she had a nice shape. Finding a buyer for her would be easy.

At her first auction in '86, she was sold to a business man from Tshikapa. He took her into the nearby 'sample' room and she was compliant as she knew she would be returned to a farmer if she was not. He was very happy and they returned to his home with two other girls in his harem.

At his home, she discovered that her sole purpose was to please him and any of his business partners who visited his home. He had a wife who knew and approved of the arrangement and she treated the harem well and made sure they were healthy. She did not mind her husband pleasing himself, but she did not want any diseases he might catch.

But, there was a dark side to her 'perfect' life. Over the eight years she was a member of this harem, she had four children. Once she gave birth, the babies were taken and she never found out what happened to them. But, the merchant's wife made sure the pregnant girls were fed well and healthy and Anana assumed the children were taken and sold to adoption agencies. Many foreign celebrities liked to adopt abandoned babies and Anana hoped that was their fate.

But, it was 1994 and Anana was 30 years old and was not tight like the new girls being brought in. She was sold to a slaver who took her back to Angola.

She was sold to a farmer in Calanda. Because she was attractive, he kept her in his home to help his wife. He had about 20 males slaves who worked his fields and he had another 30 female slaves of various ages. Many were pregnant or were breast feeding their female babies. The children were all female except two who were identified as the master's sons. The girls in the compound were almost all under ten or over twenty-five. Anana discovered that the slaver allowed the slaves to freely engage in sex. And, he would have many people come from the local larger towns to have sex with his girls. If there were any foreigners, he would keep track of the girls they chose and would note this when the girls got pregnant.—mixed birth slaves are easier to sell as babies.

But, not everyone was lucky. He would kill any male child born as the result of a non-foreigner pregnancy. He would buy new girls and they would work close to his home for him alone. If they got pregnant within two months, they became one of his wives. Their children would live as his. If he could not impregnate them within the allotted time, they moved to the slave quarters.

Anana got pregnant with his child. She had a boy but he died two weeks later. The master kept her for another year and she did not get pregnant again. She was sent to the quarters and was raped that evening by ten men. Later she found out that this was the normal initiation of any girls sent from the main house. She now belonged to them.

In 1996, her luck changed. A visiting buyer saw her and decided that she would be a good 'wife' and helper because of her age. He believed that, because she was older (32), she would not try to run away to her family. She was sold and went with the man from Muncondo. What she didn't know was that she was impregnated a week earlier in one of the nightly gang rapes.

The new master took her the first night in his home to show her what her role would be. His wife had to sit and watch as she knew her role. This new woman would be about her age and they would all be at his beck and call anytime. When she started to show signs of pregnancy, the master thought the baby was his. Anana had no idea who the father was and the little girl was born in '97 and named Abina, in honor of her friend.

Anana had a good life and provided him with another daughter two years later. This girl was named Alika. Until the day she was freed, they would have a decent life as slaves.

In 2006, she saw a familiar face come to her master's farm. It was her father. Jimoh had spent 28 years looking for her. In a country of death and violence, he never gave up hope. He worked to make money and used that money to move to the next location he heard she might be. He lost her when she was in the Congo but someone knew she had been sold and was in Muncondo.

---

# 16—Jimoh's Family Reunion

In 1977, Jimoh's daughter Anana was kidnapped by the military and he doubted he would ever see her again. But, he had to try to find her and get her back. Anana was his blood and his wife had died. Jimoh's only son had been taken by the guerrillas and he was sure by now he was dead. Anana was all he had left.

He followed her trail all over Western Angola and would use the story that he had recently married and his new wife's family owned her before and Anana was his wife's half-sister. His wife wanted her back. As a gift to his wife, he was looking for her. Many thought he was crazy but some readily helped him. Some he had to pay. Half of his leads were paid-for lies.

In most places, it worked out and Jimoh got good information. He would visit a location and talk to either the slave owner or the slave driver and get nothing. But the slaves overheard the questions. Sometimes, he would get messages from slaves that were much more reliable. These slaves knew Anana and may have lived with Anana and knew more about her than the old owner would tell.

In dealing with the guerrillas, he had to act like a former guerrilla and share tales with those who might have been in the band that took her. These he borrowed from earlier tales he had been told. Sometimes he just revealed what he observed happen in his village and described it as a participant rather than a victim.

Sometimes he wanted to just pick up the nearest gun and kill the animal who was describing raping his daughter. But he controlled his temper to get the needed information. Every tale was painful but every lead helped. The good thing about living in a violent country is that one gets many scars from cuts and gunshot wounds that lend a bit of truth to a violent lie. However, many scars are on the inside and Jimoh became hardened and heartbroken over many years. Many leads ended in a dead-end but some put him very near.

In 2006, after twenty-eight years of searching, he found his daughter. He went to the slave trader's home and talked with the man while Anana was in the adjoining room. The trader claimed he had taken her as a wife and she had bore two daughters to him. The trader claimed he loved the daughters very much and their mother and could not part with them so easily.

Jimoh learned he had two granddaughters, Abina aged 9 and Alika aged 7, but they were still the trader's property and he would not free anyone. However, he had heard the slaver say he could not 'easily' part with them. This meant he might be willing to sell them.

The slaver claimed that he could be willing to 'divorce' Anana, but Jimoh would have to pay the dowry that was never provided for the wedding. The 'dowry' for Anana would be $1000. Jimoh knew he could not pay that amount. But, the slaver continued by stating that he wanted to keep the daughters as they were his blood. He claimed that the cost of departing with two healthy young females who he cared for so deeply would be very hard and might be compensated by another $1000 or $500 each. If Jimoh did not have $2000, he might as well leave.

Anana wanted to yell out that the daughters were not the slaver's children. She could cite the rape and the timing for the elder and she could claim she was raped by his overseer while he was away. But, this could result in the girls being sold and her being sent to the farm slaves. And, if the overseer was punished, she and her girls would certainly be punished more severely.

The bottom-line was that Jimoh did not have the money. He asked if he could see his daughter and then come back later with part of the money to help convince the slaver to hold her there. The slaver agreed.

Anana was happy to see her father and they cried for several minutes while holding each other. She knew the slaver was listening and told her father that she had a good life and would be safe waiting for him to return. After about 10 minutes, the slaver's guards told Jimoh he had to leave.

Jimoh knew he had family in Lusaka and went there. He was reunited with a friend of Xhosa and she told him they needed to go to the U.S. Consulate. The friend knew of the family's situation but did not know where Xhosa was at this time. But, he said, if they went to the Consulate and told them of their family in the U.S.A. who were citizens they might get someone to help.

Since Jimoh was offered a chance to go to the U.S.A. in 1978 and Xhosa had her U.S. citizenship, the Consul's assistant listened to their story. Jimoh had details of a mission that he should not have known about and this was backed up by return messages from Langley. It was the strange offer and the non-importance of the family that intrigued the aide (a CIA operative). He included this information in his daily report and told the Consul of the situation. The Consul felt that they should wait until they heard from Langley before providing too much assistance.

The operative gave Jimoh $500 to pay the slaver and to start working for the agency in Angola. The promise was always there that the U.S.A. would help free his daughter. But, the operative was more interested in have a disposable spy than freeing a few slaves.

Jimoh spent the next two years moving back and forth in Western Angola and meeting with the Operative and a few select marines (Gunny was one of these). Everyone but Jimoh knew he was being used and the CIA operative was the only one who liked it. At one meeting, Gunny gave him another $500 that the Marines collected to make a payment.

Then, in 2009, everything changed. Obama took office and the whole administration of the Consul changed and the goal now centered on establishing good relationships with Muslim and Socialist regimes. The Consul and his 'assistant' were re-assigned. The new chief aide (Jenkins) was intrigued by the situation but Jimoh had been turned away twice by the new Consul. Jenkins arranged for a go-between to act for both of them.

On one hand, this was good because the Consul did not know the arrangement. On the other, it resulted in another person asking for Anana. The slaver assumed that Jimoh was richer than he thought and was able to send a representative. The price would go up.

When the message came in from Langley about Ball and Raymond's mission and the order to provide full support, Jenkins had to put the wheels in motion. This ended with the successful rescue and a slaver and his men rotting in hell.

When the seven returned to Lusaka, Anana and her girls were put in a hotel and Gunny got to work on finding Jimoh. It took a week and the reunion finally happened. Hugs and tears were abundant and gratitude was handed out.

Now Jimoh was with his daughter and granddaughters. He was happy and she was free after spending thirty two years of her life as a slave.

But, Jimoh owed a debt. He had to help the Americans find Xhosa. The last he had heard of her was from a friend in 2006 when they went to the Consulate.

The next step was to find Xhosa. But, first we needed to get settled and Jimoh had questions. Jimoh expressed these concerns to Jenkins.

---

# 17—*Xhosa?*

Once we got settled, Jenkins gave him the file we had. Then Jimoh took a look at the pictures on file for Mandisa. He asked us, "Are these the pictures?"

When Jenkins replied they were, Jimoh asked, "Do you have any of Mandisa? This person is not Mandisa."

I replied, "What do you mean? We know that Mandisa went to Los Angeles and was there for many years."

Jimoh replied, "I understand, but this is not Mandisa, this is Xhosa."

Jenkins asked, "After so long, how can you be sure. As far as we have heard, they were almost like twins."

Jimoh replied, "Yes, almost but not by blood and not the same. Look at the picture, Mandisa had a scar across her cheek. This picture shows no scar. Xhosa had no scar. This is Xhosa."

I thought back as hard as I could and I do recall that Mandisa always favored her right side. When they sat together, she would always be on the left. I had asked her once and she told me she hated her scar she got from a soldier and felt she would be ugly for life. Jimoh was right, this girl had no scar.

I said, "General, Jenkins . . . Jimoh is right. I remember her as a child and she did have the scar. We have been looking at Xhosa all along. I would guess that it was Mandisa who returned to Zambia, not Xhosa. We need to look for Mandisa now."

Ball contributed, "In 1982, our records show, Mandisa—or the one we thought was Mandisa—ran away to LA and Xhosa returned to Zambia. We came to find you to help us find any of your family including Xhosa in Zambia. But, now we need to find Mandisa it appears. Since she may have switched identities, we will search for both names."

We continued our journey and arrived back in Lusaka. Jimoh had friends there and we left him, Anana, and her daughters (Abina and Alika) with the friends. The General and I returned to our hotel and we got cleaned up and sat down to a nice meal that evening. Jenkins returned to the Consulate with Gunny. I don't know where the other guys went but I was sure we would see them if we needed them.

That evening, at dinner, we were joined by Jenkins. While we were looking for Anana, his people were also looking. His sources confirmed that 'Xhosa' Jones was no longer in Lusaka. The indications are that she has moved to Harare, Zimbabwe. She has started a business and has many business contacts. Some of those business contacts do business in Zambia. Finding her was actually very easy because she is very high profile.

In the morning, we met up with Jimoh and the others. We told him that we know where Mandisa using the name of Xhosa is and we will go there next week. We needed to wait for the State Department to issue U.S. Passports for all of them. Upon hearing this, Anana was very happy and told her daughters.

The families had a nice visit and Ball and I had a short vacation. Jenkins went back to work keeping his boss in line. Gunny? Gunny did what Marines do—his job. It was a short week. The passports were ready and all the airline tickets were bought and hotel reservations made. Getting the ladies on a plane was a little difficult, but when they saw so many boarding, it became easier.

The one thing in the back of my mind was 'what is Jimoh thinking'. He must realize that the U.S. Government is spending a lot of money and time and effort to help a few unimportant Angolans. Why? That will come later, if he asks.

When we landed, we were met by Jenkins' counterpart from the U.S. Embassy. He had five vehicles, a Marine driver and guard in each, a government representative and a local politician waiting for us. The government representative seemed to be confused by the presence of the Africans in our party but they had U.S. Passports which also made it more confusing.

Jenkins explained that they were U.S. citizens from Atlanta, Georgia who were interested in expanding their business with Ms. Jones. They were a couple and their daughters. Ball and I were financial backers and friends of the family. This all seemed to fit in and Jimoh and Anana allowed us to do the talking when either of the men asked a question.

The government and businessmen knew Ms. Jones and were not too happy with her desires to help others, but were very happy to take the money she brought to the city. They would help us but did not like it.

We were driven toward Harare Polytechnic on A5. Xhosa/Mandisa owned a book store "Future by the Book" on Prince Edward Street near the college. She was using her U.S. citizenship to get business tax breaks and to import items cheaper and faster from Atlanta based companies. For all intents and purposes, she was affluent in a city of middle class and poor. She spread her wealth and had many single women and orphans working for her and staying nearby in an apartment building she bought. Getting her to leave would be almost impossible. We might have to tell her the truth. Her desire to help others would be our ace in the hole.

When the five vehicles pulled up and occupied the spaces that had been kept clear for us, Mandisa/Xhosa and some employees came outside. She immediately knew the Embassy was involved and was perplexed. Then she saw Jimoh. She jumped in the air and screamed and ran to him. The others called his name, not out of familiarity but out of stories they had been told.

Jimoh looked closely at her and said, "You are Xhosa? We thought you were Mandisa using your name. Please, play along. Raven and Grunt are here to help you and others. Act like you know them and the girls."

Xhosa said she understood. When they broke their long embrace, she yelled "Uncles, I have not seen you in so long." She ran to us and gave us a hug and kiss on the cheek. "How is Atlanta?" She did not wait for an answer and ran to the ladies. She spoke in their dialect and there was a lot of hugging and kissing. Everyone was a good actor. If this was a movie, Oscars would be plentiful.

Xhosa took us inside and introduced us to her employees and told us there would be a feast tonight. She sent a couple ladies out with instructions and everyone was full of smiles.

Jenkins' counterpart took the lead, "Gentlemen, if we could begin our discussion? I am sorry Ms Jones but these gentlemen are busy and need to get back."

Xhosa replied, "Yes, we can talk back here." She took us to a large room with a table. I am sure it was their lunchroom. While watching her ad lib, I was amazed at how adept she was at saying the right thing while knowing nothing. She knew we were there for a very important reason but we had to have a cover. She played along and deserved the previously mentioned Oscar.

Jimoh and his family were taken to Xhosa's home. The girls needed a rest and the fewer actors in our play, the better.

We sat down and some girls brought us bottled water and hot tea. Jenkins continued, "We have come here to try to expand this business, here and in other cities in Zimbabwe. Ms Jones and her abilities has come to the attention of my company, my card (stated as it was handed to her), and we are lucky enough to have backers who are her friends, Mr. Ball and Mr. Raymond." We all shook hands.

The proposal was that she would expand her bookstore which would employ local construction firms. Part of this would be a warehouse to store books imported from the U.S.A. and distributed to franchises. To do this, we would need to purchase the two lots next to her store. The businessman in our group was the owner of those lots and this is the first he had heard of this. When he tried to break in, the G-man stopped him and shook his head 'no' (do not interrupt). Additionally, we would need to build a dormitory on the second lot.

Since Ms Jones is known for helping the poor and homeless, she will help them, the city and the government by providing them with jobs and a place to live. We are looking at jobs to build and maintain the buildings, jobs to employ workers here and elsewhere and taxes to support government programs. Everyone wins.

The Government representative told the businessman that he would receive 50% over the value of the land and they would use his construction company. This seemed to placate him. It would appear that the operative in Harare has deep contacts in the government.

Xhosa took everything in stride but one could see that she was chomping at the bit to scream in joy. Her dreams of helping were going to come true. However, as the meeting broke up and everyone agreed to meet the following day to sign contracts, she approached Jenkins and me.

"Who are you? Why are you helping me?" she asked. "I know nothing except that my Uncle Jimoh is looking for me and then, out-of-the-blue, you all show up and have a plan in place and scheme that affects my life and my friends. I am very confused and concerned."

"Xhosa, you may not remember me." I began, "I am Raven and you use to sit on my lap and laugh for hours in the short time we were together. I know we did not visit in America. But, you have to trust us. There are things we cannot tell you. It does not involve any danger to you or your friends. But, it could ultimately help many people and will definitely help these and others in the future. Please, trust us."

Xhosa took my hand, "The men who saved my family are my family. You were one of those men. I trust you. I do not trust the businessmen and government here, but it seems they have been bought." We laughed. "Now, let's prepare for dinner." We all left.

The evening's celebration was simple food but elaborate preparations. Xhosa's home was the second floor on the apartment building she bought. The rest of the building's upper four floors had six apartments each and about 90 women and children. She did have some close friends who stayed with her and one seemed 'closer' than the others. The only males were young children. The dinner was long and the talk was pleasant—mostly between Jimoh and Xhosa. However, Xhosa and Anana did get reacquainted.

During dinner, I asked Jimoh about the identity error. He said that he also did not understand. Mandisa had a scar and the girl in the picture looked like her but had no scar. I talked with Jenkins and he said the Agency would evaluate the photo and see what they could find out.

Once Jimoh and Xhosa are finished with their celebration, we called Jimoh over and informed him we need to take Xhosa back to America. We needed him to try to persuade her to come for a short time.

Jimoh asks, "Why is she so important to America? She is only one girl. She has so much she wants to do here and will want to plan the construction."

We take Jimoh into another room and we explain the whole situation to him. We tell him why we came to find him and Xhosa and any other potential relatives. We explained that the lives of millions may be saved by Xhosa because she was Mandisa's sister.

"But," Jimoh says, "Xhosa was not Ummi and Abu's daughter."

I could not have been hit with a Mack truck any harder than that comment. I asked, "What do you mean? Ummi always called her daughter and the girls look so much alike, almost twins."

Jimoh explained, "Yes. Ummi saved Xhosa when she was a baby. We had some refugees who were staying with us in our village on their way to Zambia. The next day, the soldiers came. Xhosa's mother was a young widow and had family in Zambia. Xhosa's mother was young and attractive and the only such female in our village when they came, the others were out in the fields or collecting water. Xhosa's mother was minding the children and the fires. The soldiers beat the old people, one cut Mandisa for crying—that is when she got her scar—and they took Xhosa's mother for their service. All of this, I learned when my family and I arrived a month later."

Ball asked, "So you are saying that Xhosa is not a blood relative?"

"That is correct, and I have no information on her family except for maybe having relatives in Zambia. If you are looking for them, I cannot help and neither can Xhosa. She was only a baby and would not even know what I am telling you now. As far as she knows, she is Ummi's daughter."

We took some time to process this information and to decide what we could do. It seems as though we have no way to find Xhosa's family and we no longer need to. And there is no way to find a cure without telling the government of Zambia to run blood tests on their entire population. But it would only show up if they were Jimoh's relatives. It appears that Xhosa would be staying in Zimbabwe. We do have four girls from Anana and possibly Jimoh's son still living with possible offspring in Angola. I doubt getting any cooperation there would be possible.

Jenkins was sure that the CIA and CDC could come up with 'something' that would result in blood tests and the discovery. But, would the Zambians cooperated? Would it create panic and an exodus from the country–including her family? Would they find a cure?

However, we did come up with a solution we all agreed upon. We gathered Jimoh, Anana, her daughters and Xhosa. Jenkins told them, "The U.S.A. has already made Xhosa a citizen and she may readily return. We have also made all of you U.S. citizens. We would like to take all of you back with us. You will be given relocation assistance and citizenship. All we ask is that you let us do a complete physical exam on you when we return and provide you with any medical assistance you need."

Anana and her daughters were ecstatic. Xhosa nodded and mouthed 'thank you, God' but we knew she was remaining. Jimoh came to me and said, "You want to see if we have Mandisa's blood?"

"Yes," I replied quietly. "I am sure there is only a slim chance but still a chance. You are Abu's brother and if Mandisa got her blood from Abu, then you may be the key." I turn and walk back to Ball and Jenkins.

Anana, seeing that frown on her father's face, comes to Jimoh and asks, "Father, aren't you happy? We are all going to America to have a new life."

Jimoh looks at her and quietly says, "Daughter, our survival is based on a lie. We are going to America because they believe we are related to Mandisa. They believe I am Abu's brother. For you and your daughters, please never tell them that Abu and I were not related. They do not understand the use of the words 'uncle' and 'aunt' in our culture. Remain silent. The U.S.A. will spend a lot of money to find your brother and your daughters. They will do what we cannot."

She did not understand the need to be related to Mandisa, but she understood the request from her father. She will remain silent.

---

# 18—Back in L. A.

At a blood bank in Los Angeles, two clerks are going through their files. They have been tasked with checking their stores and destroying expired stock. The first clerk takes a frozen packet and says, "Jones, Mandisa, auto-transfusion, June 2008."

The second replies, "What was the procedure that was scheduled?"

The first looks at the file and replies, "Her file doesn't say. But, there appears to be two units here. I will call her clinic and ask them if we still need this."

She calls the clinic and the clerk looks at her records. She tells the blood bank, "Mandisa came here in '98 for a facial scar removal. From her record, she decided in May '08 that she wanted a boob job. We suggested she do an auto-transfusion for the surgery as a precaution. She came in a few times to let us know she was still interested. But, we haven't seen her in over a year. Go ahead and use it for someone else, we will tell her she has to begin again if she comes in."

The clerk removes the 'auto-transfusion' label and placed the two units in the general use refrigerator. She closes the fridge, walks across the room, turns off the light and exits.

The End?

---

# Main Characters

James "Grunt" Ball—Green Beret First Lieutenant; now a Lieutenant General and decorated veteran of 34 years and former Division Commander.

Robert "Raven" Raymond—Staff Sergeant, Airborne Infantry, 82nd Airborne Division; retired as Sergeant Major in 1996.

David "Tennessee" Reed—Sergeant First Class, Airborne Infantry, 82nd Airborne Division; retired as Command Sergeant Major in '96; Died of Abdominal cancer in 2008.

Gary "Cat" Kiddy—Staff Sergeant, Airborne Infantry, 82nd Airborne Division; Killed in action in Grenada.

Mike "Street" Lane—Staff Sergeant, Airborne Infantry, 82nd Airborne Division; left the military to pursue a real estate career; killed in an armed robbery while showing a home in '87.

Harry "Company" Fuhrman—CIA Operative; Killed in action thought to have occurred in Yemen.

Mandisa Jones—32 yr-old Prostitute in 2008 after 16 years on the street (1992-2008)—Arrived in America as a political refugee in 1978.

Abu and Ummi Jones—Father died in '93 and Mother died in '95.

Xhosa Jones—now 33 years old and somewhere in Zambia after leaving the USA in '92. Discovered as a business woman in Harare, Zimbabwe.

Anana—now 46 year old daughter of Jimoh. Taken in Angola in '77 at the age of 13. Escaped a year later but taken into indentured servitude and traded or sold many times in Angola. She had many children of unknown fathers and only two daughters survived—now 14 (Abina '96) and 12 (Alika '98).

Jimoh—now 65 year old brother of Abu. Stayed behind in Angola to find his daughter and take her to Lusaka with their other villagers.